GETTING
RID OF
Krista

GETTING RID OF
Krista

AMY HEST

Illustrated by

JACQUELINE ROGERS

Morrow Junior Books • *New York*

Library of Congress Cataloging-in-Publication Data
Hest, Amy.
Getting rid of Krista.
Summary: With the help of her friend, Hank, eight-year-old
Gillie seeks a way to get her aggravating older sister to leave home.
[1. Sisters—Fiction. 2. New York (N.Y.)—Fiction. 3. Dogs—
Fiction. 4. City and town life—Fiction] I. Rogers, Jacqueline, ill.
II. Title.
PZ7.H4375Ge 1988   [Fic]   87-23981
ISBN 0-688-07149-X

J
Hest

DJ 10.95/7.94-9/88

For L.G.H., with lots of love

GETTING
RID OF
Krista

*E*VERYTHING WAS FINE and getting better. Until my sister Krista came home again. Her Greatness is eighteen, and she's supposed to be in college far away, in Boston. But fifteen days ago, Black Thursday, she came back because my father lost his job and we plain ran out of money. For the time being, anyway.

Already she's back to her nasty old habits, that Krista.

She jogs around the whole of Central Park three times a week.

She studies jazz dancing at Le Studio four times a week.

She bends and stretches every single morning, starting at six. It wouldn't be such a terrible thing to do, if only she would do it quietly and without the Record. The name of it is "Make-It, Shake-It, Shape-Up-for-You, You, You." The worst part of all is when Krista starts singing along, "It's for you-u-u-u!"

"I'm sleeping!" I try to tell her.

"And I'm toning up my body, Gillian. Haven't you heard," she sneers, "pudgy is Out, with a capital O. You-u-u-u!"

"I am *not* pudgy! And for your information, the name is Gillie, with a capital G."

"A beautiful body is just the beginning," says Krista.

"Go back to Boston." I pull the covers over my head and squish the pillow around both ears.

I wish my name were Jessica or Jenni with an *i* or Alyson with a *y* or Lindsay. There are fifteen girls and no boys in my third-grade class at the Manhattan Girls School. MGS for short. Three Jennis, two Jessicas, two Katies, two Laurens, three Alysons, and then there's me.

I do not belong in a snooty place like MGS. Here's why.

I'm the only one with a name like Gillian.

I'm the only one who wears jeans or corduroys all the time. The Jennis, Laurens, and all the rest think they're off to a party every day of their lives with their bright rhinestone dresses and fringed skirts from Madison Avenue.

I'm the only girl whose parents are old. Not falling-on-the-floor old but sort of middle-aged. My mother doesn't own a pair of leather pants, and my father's hair is white in spots. All the other fathers come around in jeans with a crease from the cleaners and new Nike sneakers. Mine wears tweedy jackets. Even in summer.

I'm the only one whose best friend is a boy.

I'm the only one whose sister is old enough to be in college. Worse yet, I'm the only one whose sister is back.

*I*T WAS MY MOTHER who told me Krista would be coming back home for a while.

"Home here?" I couldn't believe my ears.

"Home here."

I yelled a nasty word or two. I stamped my foot, hard, on the kitchen floor. I reminded her how it's my room now, all of it. I reminded her how happy Krista would be down in the Village at Aunt Marcy's place.

"Krista will sleep in her own bed." My mother wasn't fooling around. "She will have to get a part-time job, too. With luck," she added, "we'll have her back to Boston by September."

"September!" I squeaked. "September is like forever!"

My mother tossed salad in the bowl. "Let's hope your father finds work by then." And she gave me one of those I'm-counting-on-you looks and said, "I'm counting on you, Gillie."

"Me? Why me? I'm only nine," I said.

"*You've* got common sense. You were born with it." My mother frowned. "Krista may be eighteen, but when it comes to maturity . . . well . . ."

So I stood a little straighter and helped myself to a cherry tomato. "If you ask me," I said, "Krista's biggest problem is her looks. Too much of a good thing, if you know what I mean."

My mother stopped her tossing and said, "I do know what you mean."

Krista is beautiful and everybody knows it. Especially Krista. Ordinary sisters want to be doctors or teachers, park rangers or bank tellers. Not Krista. *She's* going to be an actress, of course. A Broadway star . . . movie idol . . . rich . . . famous . . . dazzling.

Nobody—and I mean nobody—wants a beautiful sister who is destined for Broadway *and* Hollywood. No matter what they tell you. No matter how much they seem not to care. Even if they pretend to like her a little, what they really want is for her skin to break out in a mysterious rash . . . her nose to grow long and pointy . . . her hair to start falling to the floor in big blond clumps . . .

So far none of this has happened to Krista. She never even had a pimple.

Her Greatness is a pain. No doubt about it.

I LIVE AT 340 Central Park West. Manhattan. This used to be a pretty regular neighborhood, but lately it's getting a little too fancy to suit me. Take my father's old-time barbershop. Overnight it turned into a glitzy café serving spicy Thai dishes with names I can't pronounce. And my mother's favorite deli? A tofu/yogurt bar, of all things. Good-bye, meatball heros. . . .

My best friend, Hank, a regular not a fancy person, lives in the same building. I live in 3C, and he lives in 4C. The girls at MGS don't know about Hank, which is just the way I want it. He's just not the sort of friend you feel like sharing with a bunch of girls in rhinestone dresses.

I mean, how do you explain a boy with reddish-brown hair that usually needs cutting, pale blue glasses that slide down his nose, and no shoes at all but seven pairs of sneakers—Monday reds, Tuesday blacks, Wednesday greens, and so on?

Hank's father drives a taxi, and sometimes he doesn't get home until three o'clock in the morning. Hank says the key to success with your parents is to *keep talking*. So on those nights when his father works late, Hank leaves tape-recorded messages on their kitchen table. Last week he even recorded our trip to the emergency room.

"Hi Dad, this is Hank, your son. Time: 4:30 P.M. I'm bleeding all over this guy's cab, but he says he understands, he's got kids, too. My left knee got gashed open in the playground just now, but don't you worry. Mom keeps squeezing my hand and telling me everything is fine, but I think she's on the verge of passing out. You know Mom! Gillie's no better. She says she'll throw up if I show her my knee one more time, but it's hard to resist. . . . I've never seen so much blood, but don't you worry. . . ."

Hank's mother is taking a course to sell real estate. She took it once before, but this time she intends to pass. She wears high heels all the time, even on weekends, and Hank says she also intends to make a pile of money.

My mother makes a little money. She works in Bloomingdale's. Gloves.

*B*REAKFAST IS NOT the calmest meal in my house. My mother doesn't smile. My father's always late. And now that Her Greatness Krista is back, there's a whole new person butting into my business. Take today.

Five minutes after seven. I come flying to the table. "Can I have chocolate in my milk?" I ask, closing up my book bag.

"No," says my mother.

"You'll get pimples," warns my sister.

"No one asked you, Krista!"

"Quiet!" says my father.

I try again. "Can I have a little coffee in my milk?"

"Coffee!" hoots my sister.

"You're late, eat your toast," says my mother. She pushes two slices, black around the edges, in front of me.

Her Greatness Krista doesn't have to drink milk anymore. She doesn't eat raspberry jelly or cinnamon toast, either, all because of her beautiful body and her silky skin. What a bore! She eats one three-minute egg every day for fifteen days and says she even likes it.

My father turns to Krista. "It's time to look for a job."

"I will," she promises. Sweet as sugar.

"Today." When he hands her the help-wanted pages, I feel like shouting, "Yippee, yippee, yippee."

Instead I say, "Don't you guys know Krista's going to be a star? An actress-to-be can't go to *work*, for goodness sake!"

My mother sips black coffee standing up. She never sits at breakfast, even on Sunday. "This star will get a job," she says, "so she can go back to college next September."

Krista waves just-polished nails in the air. "What do you want me to do, bag groceries at the A&P?"

"Her Greatness does not bag groceries," I say solemnly.

"I'll get you a job folding sweaters in Bloomingdale's," my mother offers.

"Her Greatness does not fold sweaters." I lick raspberry off the whole of my pinkie. "She drops them, on the floor."

My father gives me a warning look. Then he tucks his *Wall Street Journal* into three even sections. He always does that when he is going to say something important at breakfast. "No more stalling, Krista. You have to get a job. We both have to get jobs," he adds unhappily.

"Well, nobody hires a person with dirty hair." Krista sighs. "I'd better go wash mine."

"She already did that," I whisper as she floats out of the room.

Krista takes three showers a day. At least. One in the morning, right after her session with the Record. One before dinner. And one right before she slips into bed. I don't know why she has to be so clean. I take one shower a day, and even at MGS, where some people say I'm unconventional, nobody says I smell.

$\mathcal{H}$ANK HAS TWO DOGS and two goldfish. I've never understood the thrill of goldfish, but he thinks they're neat. They live on his dining room table, in a see-through bowl with gravel on the bottom. Hank can sit and watch them by the hour. I think anything more than thirty-one seconds is a waste of time. And extremely boring.

His dogs are a different story, though. English pointers. Not a trace of mutt anywhere. An old man in a gray flannel suit left them in the back seat of his father's cab. That was two years ago. And he ran, that old man, fast, into Grand Central Station, calling over his shoulder, "They're all yours, buddy! Good luck!"

16

Hank and I spend a lot of time walking Buster and Keaton in Central Park, which is right across the street from our building. You're not supposed to let your dog run wild in New York, so mostly they stay on long leather leashes. The one bad part is, you have to scoop or you get a fine.

This morning we take them into the park at Ninetieth Street, as we do every morning before school. It's my turn to scoop, since Hank did it yesterday.

"I can't wait for Krista to go back to college. She gets to be a bigger pain every single day," I complain.

Hank unhooks leashes and then starts chasing the dogs around fat tree trunks. They leap playfully and yelp and wag their tails.

I run along. "My father says she's got to go to work while she's in New York. But, of course, Her Greatness is too great for that!"

"Why doesn't she bag groceries at the A&P?" Hank calls out from behind a bush.

"Oh, sure."

"How could I forget?" he jokes, smacking his forehead. "Girls who look as good as Krista don't go in for grocery work!"

"That's not funny."

Hank throws two sticks across the open field. "Give a guy a break!" he pleads as Buster and Keaton take off.

"*I'm* the one who needs a break. *I'm* the one with Krista for a sister." I sigh. "We've got to get her out of town." I sigh again. "But that takes money."

Hank twists his mouth around. He takes off his glasses and rubs his eyebrows.

"None of this would have happened if my father hadn't lost his job at the university. It's not fair!" I shout.

"*My* father says life isn't fair, and the sooner you figure it out, the better off you are." Hank sounds smart. "By the way, Gillie, if money is the key to getting Krista out of town, why don't *you* try to raise some?"

"Who, me?"

Buster drops a stick at our feet. Hank bends to

pick it up and to retie his black sneaker lace. "You'd need my help, of course. But don't you worry, Gillie, I'll think of something."

Keaton skids into me. I rub his head and say to Hank, "I'm counting on you."

"You always count on me." He clips the dogs to their leashes. "Meet me at the Ice Cream Emporium at four." He checks his watch. "That gives me eight hours to come up with a plan."

"I'll be there."

"And bring money," he says. "Your treat today."

As I head for the crosstown bus and school, I wave to Hank . . . and blow an imaginary farewell kiss to Her Greatness Krista.

ESIDES THE ICE CREAM, the best part about the Ice Cream Emporium is the teenagers who work there. They're nothing like my sister. *These* teenagers are nice, and they even like kids. I know because sometimes they give me a double scoop for the price of one.

Hank eats pistachio with rainbow sprinkles. Always. I eat coffee with chocolate sprinkles. Always.

"We'll walk dogs!" he shouts when I push open the door at four o'clock. "We'll walk dogs and give the money to Krista!"

"All of it?"

Hank closes his eyes. He nods his head. "All of it," he says. "The faster we hand her a pile of

21

money, the faster she's out of town. Then maybe
you'll smile once in a while, the way you used to."

The girl behind the counter gives us our cones.
Her little blue eyes are friendly, and she's gracious
enough to say thanks when I hand her money, even
though I'm short a nickel.

We sit side by side on our favorite bench along the
wall. Even though it's the middle of February, and
freezing cold outside, plenty of people stop by.
Hank and I like to size them up, making penny bets
on the flavors they will choose. So far this month
Hank owes me fourteen cents. I owe him twenty-
five.

"We can make a dollar fifty an hour." Hank pops
the last drop of ice cream into his mouth. He cleans
his glasses with a paper napkin. "That is, a dollar
fifty for each dog."

"And where are we supposed to find all the dogs?"

"In our building. There must be a million," he
says.

"What about Buster and Keaton, wouldn't they be
jealous?"

"They'll love the company." Hank grins. "Maybe we'll even find them a couple of girlfriends."

"Are you sure we have to give Krista every single penny?"

Hank waves his hands around impatiently. "Pay attention, would you, Gillie? If we walk five in the morning and five after school . . ."

"After school?" I say. "What about playtime? I'm a kid, Hank, I need to play!"

"Like I said, if we walk five in the morning and five after school, that's ten a day. Fifteen dollars!"

"Fifteen." I whistle. "Pretty good."

"And don't forget weekends."

"Weekends, too?" I wail.

"We need the bucks," he says, "in order to get rid of Her Greatness once and for all."

I think about that.

"I knew you would see it my way." Hank pulls a notebook from his backpack. "Let's make a sign. We'll never get customers if we don't advertise."

After chewing on my pencil awhile, this is what I write:

23

IS IT A BOTHER TO RUN AFTER YOUR HOUND BEFORE
  WORK?
ARE YOU SICK AND TIRED OF SCHLEPPING AROUND
  YOUR FOUR-LEGGED FRIEND AFTER WORK?
KICK OFF YOUR SHOES ... LET US DO SOMETHING
  NICE FOR YOU!

CALL DOG WALKERS BY DESIGN. BEST PRICE IN TOWN:
  $1.50 PER WALK.
  ASK FOR GILLIE AND HANK, YOUR GOOD NEIGH-
  BORS IN 3C AND 4C

We add our telephone numbers, and Hank says
it's brilliant. I think so, too. We hang the sign on the
lobby bulletin board.

Then we run up the back stairs, me to 3C and
Hank to 4C, and wait for the phone to ring.

I SIT ON A HIGH step stool inches from the kitchen phone. It doesn't ring, even once. After fifteen minutes I call Hank.

"Any prospects?"

"Not yet. Keep the faith," he says, and hangs up.

Then comes Krista, a little sweaty but all decked out in black tights, purple leg warmers, a long-to-her-knees sweater, and jazz shoes. She drops her dance bag on the counter, reaches for a carrot, snips off the ends, but doesn't bother to scrape.

"You ought to scrape," I say.

"Too hungry." She chomps hard. "Want one?"

I shake my head. "I like mine scraped."

Krista finishes the carrot. She arches her back.

Blond hair sweeps the floor. "Jazz dancing makes me sing!" she sings.

"Did you get a job?"

"These things take time." She jumps to her feet.

"Daddy says you've got to get a job."

Her Greatness is so busy whipping around in circles, she doesn't seem to hear me.

"So you'd better get one," I say a little louder.

Suddenly she is at my side. And she towers over me. "I'm going to tell you something, Gillian." Krista's tone has a certain edge. *"Mind your own business!"*

"This *is* my business."

"It is not!"

"Why don't you just quit pretending you're some great actress," I sneer, "and get yourself a proper job!"

"Who asked you?" she shouts.

"If you *don't* go back to college, Krista, Mom and Daddy will feel like a couple of crumbs for the rest of their lives!" (I make up most of that, but probably there is some truth in it, too.)

Anyway, for the first time in half an hour she stops shimmying.

"You'll never get back to Boston on good looks alone," I say in my nicest, kindest voice. "It takes money. . . ."

The telephone rings. Even as I pick it up, Hank is talking. "Someone called," he says. "16 F. Brand-new in the building and she's got a dog."

I smile into the telephone.

"She wants to meet us, Gillie. *Now*."

ANK RAPS the brass knocker. Inside, loud barks. Louder than any
barks I've ever heard. Ever.

"Big mistake." I head for the stairwell.

Hank latches on to my wrist. "It's *little* dogs that
make all the noise," he says. "Everyone knows that."

A lady in yellow opens the door, and the biggest
blur of fur I've ever seen, anywhere, is running at
me. I back into the wall, squeeze my eyelids tight,
and wait. Will it eat me whole, I wonder, or take
little bits of me . . . bite by bite by bite?

"You must be the dog walkers." The lady smiles.
"I'm Alberta Sullivan. Come in, we'll chat."

28   I am pinned to the wall, but no one seems to

notice. Hank steps into the apartment. "Coming, Gillie?"

I don't move a muscle. I don't breathe, either.

But I am saved. Alberta Sullivan claps her hands. "Tiny Sullivan!" she scolds in a high-pitched voice. "You leave that nice girl alone and come into this house!"

We're invited to sit on a raggedy brown couch. It creaks and sags as we settle into opposite corners. Mrs. Sullivan sits in the middle, and Tiny squirms around until she fits under the glass coffee table. She never takes her eyes off me, that dog—even once. And her tail makes a terrible thumping on the wood floor.

"Tea?" Mrs. Sullivan offers.

Hank shakes his head politely.

She turns to me. "Tea, dear?"

"Only when I'm sick."

Hank gives me a dirty look. "What Gillie means is, she never drinks tea before supper." Then he gives me the dirty look again.

Mrs. Sullivan climbs over my knees to get to the kitchen. As soon as she's out of sight, I say, "Let's get out of here!"

"We need the bucks." Hank talks without moving his lips.

"But that dog . . . a monster . . ."

"Here I am!" Mrs. Sullivan chirps like a bird. "I need my tea, I do." She dangles her steaming cup high over my head to get to the middle of the couch again.

"We'd like the job," says Hank.

Mrs. Sullivan holds an Oreo cookie underneath the coffee table. It disappears fast. "You would like to walk my Tiny?"

"We have fine credentials," says Hank.

"You would take good care of my Tiny?"

"Oh, yes!" I give a friendly little wave to her Tiny, just to prove it.

"Lovely!" Mrs. Sullivan claps her hands.

"We can start tomorrow." Hank tells her. "Eight-o'clock pickup. If you like our work, we'll even come back again before supper."

"I will pay you a dollar."

"A dollar fifty," I say. "The sign says a dollar fifty."

Alberta Sullivan stiffens. "I pay a dollar."

"A dollar it is." Hank stands up.

"But Hank! We agreed—"

"Let's go, Gillie." He pushes his glasses way up his nose.

The second I stand up, Tiny stands up, too. I walk slowly to the front door. Tiny does, too. I put my hand on the doorknob, very carefully. Tiny lunges forward and I scream. Then Tiny does the strangest thing. She slobbers all over my fingers, every one of them.

Hank gives me a push out the door, then closes it behind us. I slide to the floor. He sits beside me.

"Cheer up," he says. "We got the job!"

"She's supposed to pay a dollar fifty." I wipe my soaked hand across the seat of my jeans.

There must be an easier way than this to run my sister out of town.

"WE'RE IN DOGS," I announce at the dinner table.

"Dogs?" My mother drops a slice of cold meat loaf on my plate. It is way too pink and horrible to look at.

"Dog *walking.*" I reach for the ketchup and start pouring. "Hank and I are going to make a ton of money."

"Since when do third-graders need a ton of money?" Krista dips into her meat loaf as if it were filet mignon.

"I had a good interview this morning," my father says quietly.

My mother's fork stops midway to her mouth. 33

"They will call—soon, let's hope." He turns to Krista. "Did you have any luck today?"

She flips her ponytail. "I was pretty busy with my jazz classes, so I didn't get a chance to look. . . . I might just as well keep in shape," she adds, "while I'm stuck in New York."

"I'm glad about your shape, Krista, but you need to get a job," says my mother.

"These things take time." Krista stares at the kitchen clock.

"We want you back in college, young lady, and we need your help to get you there!" My mother is talking with her hands. She always does that when she's trying to get through to Her Greatness.

"Even Gillie wants to help," my father points out.

"Who, me?"

"Imagine, walking dogs to see her family through a hard time," he goes on.

I smile across the table at Her Greatness. "And I've decided to give every single penny I make to Krista," I say in my adorable-child voice.

34   "Why?" She frowns suspiciously.

"Because I love you."

Then I have to excuse myself. And barely make it out of the room before I burst out laughing.

*T*INY DRAGS ME through the lobby. And out the front door. "Help, Hank!"

"Hang on!" he calls as he zips Buster and Keaton into matching sweaters.

I half gallop, half slide. Just outside our building, Tiny swerves past a big man in a black uniform. She goes one way and I go the other.

"Hey, quit!" cries the big man. Tiny's leash is wrapped like a lasso around his ankles.

"Gosh, mister, I'm sorry. . . ."

Hank runs over. "I told you, Gillie, we've got to teach Tiny some manners."

So I start yelling. "What's the matter with you, dog!"

But Tiny isn't paying attention to me. What she is

paying attention to is the dark blue limousine parked at the curb. Standing tall on hind legs, she licks at the window and waves her tail around in furry circles.

"Are you the police?" I ask the big man.

"Chauffeur." He straightens his cap. "Jackie Duke to you, but my boss calls me Jacques."

"Chauffeur!" I whistle. "This neighborhood gets fancier by the day."

Buster and Keaton sniff the car door.

"Whose limo is it?" asks Hank.

"Murray Bromo's."

Hank's eyes open wide. So does his mouth. "Murray Bromo, the famous Broadway producer?"

"The one and only."

"You mean, someone that famous lives right here in our building?"

"Penthouse. But don't tell your friends," warns Jackie. "Mr. Bromo keeps a modest profile."

I lower my voice. "Is he in the car?"

"*That* is Pierre." Jackie sticks out his tongue.

I peek inside. A small white dog, curly from top to

bottom, sits on the back seat. "So that's why Tiny's going crazy. She's got a crush on a poodle called Pierre!"

"Maybe Tiny would like to *elope* with Pierre." Jackie snorts. "That's one way to get the little so-and-so out of my hair."

Hank takes a look. "Cute dog."

"Cute, my eye!" He snorts again. "All of a sudden, out of the blue, Mr. Bromo decides I'm such a nice guy, I should have the pleasure of taking his pride and joy for his morning constitutional. Half an hour in the fresh air, he says, every single day.

"The thing he doesn't say is that his pride and joy *hates* fresh air. After his number one, the little pain in the neck refuses to walk another step. Won't budge."

Hank passes around sticks of gum. "I never heard of a dog who doesn't like a good old run in the park."

"He's allergic to grass," Jackie explains. "I'm fed up. From now on, if Pierre doesn't walk when I say walk, he can sit it out in the back seat."

"What does Mr. Bromo say about that?"

Jackie looks scared. "If he finds out, I'm fired."

Hank cracks his gum. He double-knots long red sneaker laces. "I know what Pierre needs."

"Me, too." Jackie makes a fist.

"Pierre needs *professional* dog walkers." Hank winks at me. "Take me to your leader," he says to Jackie. "Take me to Murray Bromo!"

"I WISH I WENT to school with Hank," I confide to Krista.

She is lounging on her bed. Glossy photos are everywhere.

"I just don't fit in at Manhattan Girls," I go on. "They're the biggest bunch of snobs."

Krista stares at her pictures. "You've got a scholarship, Gillie. You get *A*'s in everything. Besides, it's one of the best schools in the city. Don't forget, I went there, too."

"You mean I could turn out like you!"

She flies off the bed. "Take it back," she orders, twisting my arm behind me. "Say something nice, something wonderful about your sister."

"My sister . . . you . . . are beautiful and a great

dancer and a super jogger and you're going to be a star . . . help!" I cry out.

She lets go. "You forgot to say what a marvelous singer I am." She plops onto her bed again.

"And you're a marvelous singer, too."

Once in a while—and I mean once in a *great* while—Krista and I can have a really nice time together. When she talks to me like I'm a real person and not just a pain in the butt, that's when I like her. A little bit, anyway.

"Don't worry about the snooty girls. Just find something you're good at," she recommends, "the way I found Drama Club."

"But I can't act or dance, and I'm not pretty like you. . . ."

She pins an eight-by-ten picture of herself to the wall. "What do you think?"

I kneel beside her. "Fabulous." I touch it with my fingertips. "You look like a movie star."

"I was hoping you would say that." Krista sighs. "You are the only one in this family who believes in me."

"I am?"

"All Mom and Daddy care about is college. They don't understand I really do intend to be an actress."

"Even movie stars go to college," I remind her.

Krista works on her cuticles, pushing them back and back. "I really do intend to be an actress," she repeats quietly. "The sooner, the better."

"But Boston!" I cry. "You love Boston!"

Krista gives me one of her slow smiles. I have a sneaking suspicion I'm about to hear something I don't want to hear. "Now that I'm back in New York," she says, "I realize this is where I want to be."

I inhale. I exhale. I consider punching her in the nose.

Then Her Greatness does the most amazing thing. She throws her arms around my neck and gives me the biggest kind of hug. Under the circumstances there's nothing left to do but hug her back.

But one thing is certain. I'm not giving up. Krista's got to go.

"I'M SCARED, Hank."

"The worst Murray Bromo can do is tell us to get lost. Remember, Gillie, we need the business." Hank pushes the penthouse buzzer. "Let me do the talking."

The door opens slowly. A short man in a long green robe (silk, I think) and little red slippers (suede, maybe) stands there frowning at us. He has navy blue eyes and no hair at all. The top of his head is shiny, like a light bulb.

I step behind Hank.

"We don't buy Boy Scout cookies," says the man. "We're always on a diet around here." He starts to shut the door.

Hank gives a push and tumbles into the apartment. "I need to speak to Mr. Bromo," he says.

"Then speak. I am Murray Bromo and I am very busy."

"You are?"

On tiptoe, I follow the two of them into the living room. White carpet is cushy, like foam rubber, and the furniture is not the kind kids are supposed to sit on. There's real art on the walls and stacks of books with leather bindings.

Mr. Bromo points to a paisley love seat. "Sit," he says.

We sit.

He rings a little bell, and a tall man in a black tuxedo appears in the doorway.

"Bring the children a pastry, François."

François disappears. Then Pierre comes out from underneath a frilly white sofa. He leaps into my lap—like I'm his long lost mother—and licks my cheek and my chin.

"I see you like my Pierre."

"Gillie *loves* Pierre. We both do," adds Hank.

"He's not for sale, if that's why you're here."

François brings fancy pastries on a tray with doilies. They look great and smell great. I reach for one, but Hank tugs at my arm. "We've come because we want to *walk* Pierre," he tells Mr. Bromo. "Pierre is special; we knew that the minute we laid eyes on him in front of the building. He needs special dog walkers."

Pierre barks twice, then rests his head on my knees.

"Jacques takes care of that."

Pierre whimpers and whines.

"But we are professionals," says Hank, "and we only charge a dollar fifty. That's a real bargain, Mr. Bromo, sir . . ."

The telephone rings.

"Bromo here." He swings small feet onto the coffee table. "She *what*?" he shouts into the telephone. "Quit? Ran off with her boyfriend . . . to *Australia*?" He gives a loud shriek and bangs down the phone. Hard.

I jump. So does Hank.

"Professionals!" Mr. Bromo yells at us. "The word

is laughable these days . . . only I'm not laughing."
He puts his head in his hands and makes
strange wimpy noises.

"Are you all right?" I whisper.

He shakes his head. "My leading lady just quit
. . . the show opens in less than a month, and she
runs off to Australia. What is this world coming to?"

Hank licks his lips. "Looks like you'll need someone to fill in." He says it carefully. "Someone
without a boyfriend this time."

Mr. Bromo doesn't seem to hear. "Four weeks,"
he mumbles, reaching for the phone. "Where am I
supposed to find a star in four short weeks?"

"**D**ID YOU GUYS KNOW Murray Bromo lives right here in the building?" I say at dinner.

Krista rolls her eyes. "Murray Bromo lives in Paris," she says. "*Everyone* knows that." She is practically drooling.

"*Everyone* doesn't know *everything*, Greatness."

She cuts her broccoli into three dainty pieces. "You sound infantile, Gillian. Grow up!"

"Well, excuse me for living, *Gorgeous*." I collect plates noisily and stack them in the sink.

Not Krista. She never helps. She's too busy staring into her pocket mirror, smearing on the hot-pink lipstick from the fancy new drugstore on Columbus Avenue. I'll never know why she has to wear lipstick when she's eating. It rubs right off, anyway, every time she takes a bite.

"As a matter of fact, I was reading just the other day that Bromo is bringing a new show to Broadway," says my father.

"But one of his stars—" I begin.

"We saw a Bromo production on our first date!" My mother smiles at my father. "What was it called again?"

"*French Follies.*" He smiles back at her.

She puts a bowl of lime Jell-O on the table.

"I wish we had something chocolate," I mumble.

"Jello makes your nails strong," says Krista.

"That's just an old wives' tale," I tell her, looking at my nails. "Anyway, they're strong enough. I want something chocolate."

"It's bad for your complexion."

I dig my spoon into the Jell-O. It wriggles from one side of the bowl to the other, then back again to the first side. "Did you look for a job today, Krista?"

She scowls across the table at me.

"They can use your help in Bloomingdale's. I did

some checking," says my mother. "Scarves, Krista."

"Scarves!" She pounds her fist on the table. "I don't want to sell scarves!"

"You're not a child. You ought to understand," says my father. "College costs."

"*I* have a new job," I announce cheerily. "Another dog to walk. He belongs to—"

Krista stands up. "Nobody around here understands me!" she cries.

And she stomps out of the room.

"**D**ON'T FORGET the rules." François hands me one end of Pierre's leash. Rhinestones are everywhere.

Hank leans against the penthouse door. "Could you run them by us one more time?"

François clears his throat. "Never let go of the leash, even for a second. Stay on the sidewalk, never cross a street, and *never* go into that park. Pierre is allergic. And if you see a cat, grab Pierre and start running. Fast!"

"I don't know if this is worth a dollar fifty."

"If you do a good job, you can come back tomorrow."

I crane my neck to take a look inside the apartment. "How's Mr. Bromo doing? Did he find a leading lady?"

François shakes his head. "They parade through here like it's nobody's business, but Mr. Bromo can't find the right one."

"What's he looking for, anyway?"

François clears his throat. He straightens his bow tie. "Beautiful. Blond. Young. Svelte. She has to sing. She has to dance. She has to shake him up!"

"Is that all?"

I watch Mr. Bromo pace across his living room, first one way, then the other. He yells into the telephone as he goes. Every time he does an about-face, the cord twists around his waist, until he is all caught up in cord. He wears the same green robe, and those smooth little slippers. But something is different.

"Where'd he get hair?" says Hank.

"Shh!" François slams his hand across Hank's mouth. "Mr. Bromo is very sensitive about his toupee," he whispers.

I look again. Hair! Murray Bromo's got hair today . . . and lots, too.

I start to laugh. It comes right from my belly and won't stop, no matter what. "Hair today and gone tomorrow!" I sputter as Hank shoves me, and Pierre, into the elevator.

We pick up Buster and Keaton on four. They ignore Pierre. Pierre sits on his rump. He ignores them right back.

Next we collect Tiny. The minute Tiny and Pierre lay eyes on each other, I know we're in trouble. I take a look at Hank, and I know he knows it, too.

Pierre gets off his rump. Pierre is in love, for sure.

"NOW WHAT?" I shout to Hank. Buster and Keaton are flying through the lobby. Tiny flies, too, but straight at me.

Pierre does a little dance on the end of the rhinestone leash. I am holding on, but barely. Hop hop jump. Hop hop jump. His tail whips around as he moves me closer and closer to Tiny.

"Down!" yells Hank. He points a finger at Pierre's wet nose.

"You can't talk to him like that," I warn, "Mr. Bromo will kill you!" Then I start laughing all over again. Imagine telling Mr. Bromo that Pierre is in love . . . with a tall woman called Tiny. . . .

But Hank is all business. "The sooner we get these

guys walked, the sooner we get paid," he says. "We'll have to keep the two lovebirds apart. You take *him*, Gillie." Hank makes a gross face at Pierre. "I'll get a head start with Buster, Keaton, and Tiny."

I hold Pierre in my arms until they disappear into the park. "Tiny is cute and all, but probably not your type," I say.

Pierre bares teeth.

"Knock it off," I say. "Besides, you'd hurt Murray's feelings if you fell for someone with no pedigree."

I think about François's rules. There's the one about no cats . . . the one about never letting go of the leash . . . and something about allergies.

We cross to the park. "Cold?" I ask pleasantly. Pierre ignores me. Pierre has one thing on his mind, and it sure isn't the weather. He sniffs around, digging up winter weeds with manicured paws. Spraying dirt at my ankles. I throw a stick and let the leash slip to the ground. Pierre sits.

"Go for it!" I say. Pierre looks away.

I suggest a little run. Pierre doesn't like that idea, either. So I try a bit of psychology. I clap my hands and smile and tell him how handsome he is. Pierre sits. "Oh, you're really good company," I mumble, "really good." Pierre looks at the sky and howls.

Suddenly Tiny bursts through the bushes, leaping around kangaroo-style. Buster and Keaton follow, then Hank.

Pierre gets off his butt.

"What are *you* doing in the park, Gillie?" Hank jams his foot on the end of Tiny's leash. "Did you forget, Pierre is allergic to grass!"

I inhale. I exhale. Then I say, "But he never even sneezed."

Just then someone comes jogging up the road. Hank whistles. The jogger turns. It is Krista. She waves to us. Very friendly. We wave back.

Hank rubs his chin. He takes off his glasses a minute and rubs his eyebrows. "What was it Mr. Bromo is looking for in a leading lady?"

"She has to be young and beautiful and blond," I

begin. "She has to sing and dance and . . ." I stare at the back of Krista. Then I stare at Hank. "Are you thinking what I'm thinking?"

Hank smiles. "Murray Bromo may not know it, but he's about to discover his leading lady."

And I smile back. "Her Greatness, Krista."

"THE BLOOD is rushing to my brain."
Hank stands on his head between the
twin beds in my room. "This is my
best thinking position."

"Then think of a way for Mr. Bromo to discover
Krista." I sigh. "Imagine how much money she
could make on Broadway. Imagine how fast she'd be
back at college!"

Hank pulls one of those glossy photos of Krista
from underneath the bed. He blows at the dust, then
whistles. "Your sister sure is pretty."

"Don't remind me." I take two chocolates from
my desk drawer. "I'm not the one you have to sell
her good looks to."

60   "Maybe I'll slip this picture under Mr. Bromo's

door," Hank teases, "with a note that says, 'Here she is!' "

"Have a chocolate, Hank. It will settle your brain."

Hank springs to his feet. "Gotta go. My father's working late and I need to tape-record a message about the science fair. . . ."

"Tape recorder!" I snap my fingers and say it again. "Tape recorder. Why didn't I think of it sooner?"

"Think of what?" Hank frowns.

"You and I will make a tape of Krista's voice." I say it slowly. "She'll never know, of course. We'll secretly record one of her whiny little songs and somehow get it to Mr. Bromo."

"With this picture!" Hank waves it in the air. "A tape of her voice and a picture of Her Greatness!"

"Boy, are we smart." I smile.

"I'll get the machine." Hank rushes out.

I check my watch. "She'll be home any minute. Hurry, Hank! Krista always practices her singing before dinner."

"How about a little song, Krista?"

"Do you have a temperature or something?" She bends and stretches and bends and stretches. Then a couple of jazzy turns toward the long mirror. "You hate my singing," she reminds me.

"That's not true." I sit cross-legged on the bed. Hank's tape recorder makes a little bump underneath my pillow. "You have a beautiful voice, and one day you'll be a star on Broadway."

Krista stares at herself in the mirror. "Do you really think so, Gillie?"

"*Please*," I beg. "Just one little song?"

I click the "record" button.

And she starts singing. A sad song about a pretty

girl whose boyfriend dumps her for another pretty girl. I must say, Krista has a very nice voice. It is low and soft and dreamy. By the time her song is over, I could cry, because the first pretty girl is packing her bag. She's going somewhere to try to forget. Maybe even to Paris.

I click the "stop" button.

"Thanks." I hop off the bed.

"Want to hear another?" she asks.

"Not right now." I slip the tape recorder under my sweat shirt.

"Maybe they'll let me sing behind the counter in Bloomingdale's." Krista sighs. "Maybe somebody will come along and discover me right there in scarves."

"You never know where you'll be discovered." I smile at Her Greatness. "You just never know."

And I dash upstairs to 4C. Hank is waiting in the stairwell. We stuff the tape and the picture of Krista into an envelope marked FOR MURRAY BROMO, THE FAMOUS PRODUCER. PRIVATE AND CONFIDENTIAL. PLEASE OPEN RIGHT AWAY.

RANÇOIS OPENS the door. "What are you two doing here? Pierre had his evening walk already."

Hank hugs the envelope to his chest. "This is for Mr. Bromo. It's important," he says.

"Nothing is important. Except to find a star." Then François leans forward and whispers, "He's beside himself. I've never seen him quite like this."

"Who's at the door?" booms Mr. Bromo. "Another dancer who can't sing? Another singer who doesn't dance? Another actress built like last year's string bean? Who *is* it?"

"Let's beat it, Hank!" I push the elevator button. "Mr. Bromo sounds like he wants to hang someone."

"I don't hang children." Mr. Bromo stands in the

doorway. His bathrobe is wrinkled and stained with coffee. There are no slippers on his feet and no hair on his head. His shoulders sag. "Do we owe you money or something?" He walks back into his living room.

Hank follows. He takes me by the wrist. "Mr. Bromo, sir, we've found your leading lady," he says. "She sings, she dances—she even acts, I think."

"And she's pretty," I add, "like a movie star ought to be."

Mr. Bromo turns to François. "Do children always sound like this?"

Hank waves the envelope around. "It's all in here."

"Play it, Hank." I say it under my breath. "Play it!"

Hank arranges his tape recorder on the antique desk. He pushes the "play" button.

Suddenly the room fills with Krista and her sad song about the pretty girl. My eyes are glued to Mr. Bromo. He doesn't smile. He doesn't frown. He looks straight ahead, and he doesn't blink once. But when Krista gets to the last few lines, about packing up for Paris, a little tear—and I swear it's true—dribbles down his cheek.

Hank pushes the "stop" button. Then he slides Krista's picture across the desk.

Mr. Bromo takes a look. "Is she French?" he whispers.

"Nearly," Hank lies. "But more than that, she sings and dances, and as you can see, she's quite a beauty."

Mr. Bromo keeps staring at the picture. After many minutes he rushes out of the room. Pierre jumps off the paisley love seat and chews on my ankle for a while.

When Mr. Bromo comes back a few minutes later, his hair is in place. He is wearing clothes. Nice gray slacks and a bright blue shirt with a handkerchief stuffed just so in the pocket. His eyes are bright, and his shoulders don't sag.

"Take me to her," he says. "Jacques will drive. Beautiful young stars love the limo."

"We don't need the limo, Mr. Bromo."

"What Gillie means is, your star is right here in the building," says Hank. "Apartment 3C. Go on down and ring the bell."

And I smile. "Just ask for Krista."

URRAY BROMO TAKES one look at Her Greatness and practically flips.

He sits on the kitchen stool while she does a little jazz routine right past the refrigerator. He hoists himself onto the counter to listen to that sad song one more time. He doesn't smile. He doesn't frown. I think he doesn't breathe. Those navy eyes follow every twist, every turn, every high note, and every low one, too.

Krista is discovered before our very eyes.

It turns out she doesn't get the lead. Mr. Bromo shifts some roles around and gives her a part with more singing but less talking.

But she's not complaining! Even Krista never expected to be the star of the show the first time around.

Hank and I agree we've done the best possible job. And Krista treats us to triple-scoop ice-cream cones.

Because we're such good dog walkers, we go on walking Tiny and Pierre along with Buster and Keaton. We don't give a dime of it to Her Greatness, either.

Two days after Krista meets Murray Bromo, my father comes home with the best news yet. A job! A good job, too, the one he even wanted. My mother cries like crazy, the way she always does when she's extra happy.

Me? When all is said and done, I still have one small problem. It has to do with Krista. Now that she's going to be on Broadway, she will have to stick around. Boston and college are on the back burner, probably forever. Instead she will stay right here in my room, making my life more miserable than ever. And it isn't fair.

Hank says you never know; maybe Mr. Bromo's

new show will go on tour. Her Greatness Krista the
star could wind up someplace far away, after all.

Maybe even Paris!

J

Hest, Amy.

Getting rid of
Krista

CHILDREN'S LIBRARY

6-10/94

3
1/95

© THE BAKER & TAYLOR CO.